Where Will the Animals Stay?

by Stephanie Calmenson

pictures by
Ellen Appleby

Parents Magazine Press • New York

To Joanna Cole—S.C.

To Carol Bouman—E.A.

Text Copyright © 1983 by Stephanie Calmenson
Illustrations Copyright © 1983 by Ellen Appleby
All rights reserved.
Printed in the United States of America.
10 9 8 7 6 5 4

Library of Congress Cataloging in Publication Data.
Calmenson, Stephanie.
  Where will the animals stay?
  Summary: Zoo animals needing a place to stay
temporarily are offered an apartment house.
  [1. Zoo animals—Fiction.   2. Apartment houses—
Fiction.   3. Stories in rhyme]   I. Appleby, Ellen, ill.
II. Title.
PZ8.3.C13Wh   1983   [E]   83-13479
ISBN 0-8193-1119-7

Where
Will the
Animals Stay?

They're changing the zoo
At Peabody Square
From cages with bars
To fresh open air.

For animals in cages
Are sad to see.
They need lots of space;
They like to roam free.

The Keeper is ready;
The workers are too.
They will tear down the old
To make room for the new.

There's only one problem
That stands in the way:
While the workers are building . . .

They can't be set free
To roam through the street.
A lion would frighten
The people he'd meet.

Giraffes would stop traffic
Outside of the zoo . . .

No, animals everywhere
Just will not do.

The news of the zoo
Took no time to spread.
When a kind lady heard it,
She rushed there and said:

"My apartment house really
Has plenty of space.
My neighbors won't mind
A few guests at their place!"

So the animals moved
From the Peabody Zoo.
They walked in a line,
Going two by two.

The Keeper kept count
As they marched through the door.

They went straight past the doorman
And filled every floor.

He counted right up
To one hundred and three,
Then cried, "Someone's missing!
We must go and see!"

They ran across town
Asking people they met,
"Have you seen something lost,
Like a very BIG pet?"

Then back at the zoo
They found all alone
A white polar bear,
Afraid to leave home.

"Come along," said the Keeper.
"Please try to be brave."

But the scared polar bear
Would not leave his cave.

"I'll help," said the Lady.
"I've got just the thing.
I'll run home and get it.
It's easy to bring."

"This bear is my friend
From a long time ago.
Why don't you hold him.
He'll help you, I know."

And so the count went
To one hundred and four.

They filled every room
And spilled out the door.

Two in the kitchen,

Four in the den.

On the stairs there were five,

By a tub there were ten.

Now back at the zoo
They worked day and night,
Till every last thing
Was fixed up just right.

And when they were done
At the Peabody Zoo,

Together the animals
Went back two by two.

The Keeper said thanks
On behalf of them all.
"If you need *our* help,
You know where to call."

"Well now that you have
Such a nice roomy zoo,
While the workers fix our house . . .

Can we stay with you?"

About the Author

STEPHANIE CALMENSON began writing her story after talking with Ellen Appleby about the plight of Tina, the elephant. The Central Park Zoo in New York City was to be rebuilt and homes were needed for the animals. But no one would take Tina because she was known as a problem elephant.

Though her story is very different from the real one, Stephanie Calmenson says, "I hope two of the important parts of Tina's story are reflected in the book: Animals should have room to roam freely and, when there is a problem, a few kind people can help a lot."

By the time the story was finished Tina was living happily at a California zoo, where she was given plenty of room and love.